To Eric, Bobbie, and everyone at The Eric Carle Museum—
always worth the drive.

Library of Congress Cataloging-in-Publication Data
Willems, Mo.
Let's go for a drive! / by Mo Willems.—1st ed.
    p. cm.
"An Elephant and Piggie book."
Summary: Elephant Gerald and Piggie want to go for a drive, but as Gerald thinks of one thing after another that they
will have to take along, they come to realize that they lack the most important thing of all.
ISBN 978-1-4231-6482-1 (hardback)
[1. Automobile travel—Fiction. 2. Elephants—Fiction. 3. Pigs—Fiction. 4. Humorous stories.] I. Title.
PZ7.W65535Lep 2012
  [E]—dc23   2011053285

First Edition, October 2012
20 19 18 17 16 15 14 13 12
FAC-029191-18237

This book is set in Century 725/Monotype; Grilled
Cheese BTN/Fontbros; Neutraface, Fink,
Typography of Coop/House Industries

Printed in Malaysia
Reinforced binding

Visit www.hyperionbooksforchildren.com
and www.pigeonpresents.com

Let's Go for a Drive!

An ELEPHANT & PIGGIE Book

Hyperion Books for Children / *New York*
AN IMPRINT OF DISNEY BOOK GROUP

By Mo Willems

Piggie!

I have a great idea!

3

4

5

9

13

17

Bringing sunglasses on a drive is smart planning.

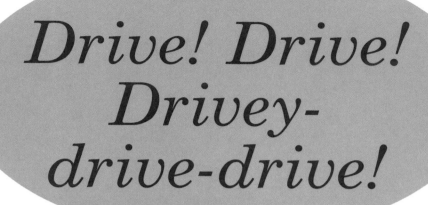

21

24

Make a plan and
stick to it, is what I say.

28

30

34

37

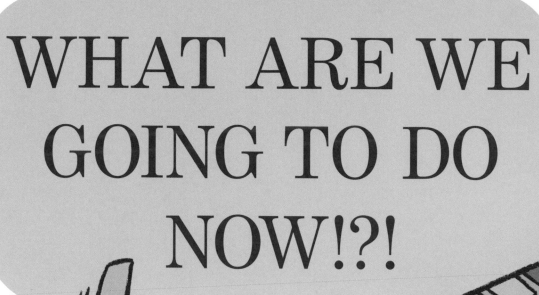

52

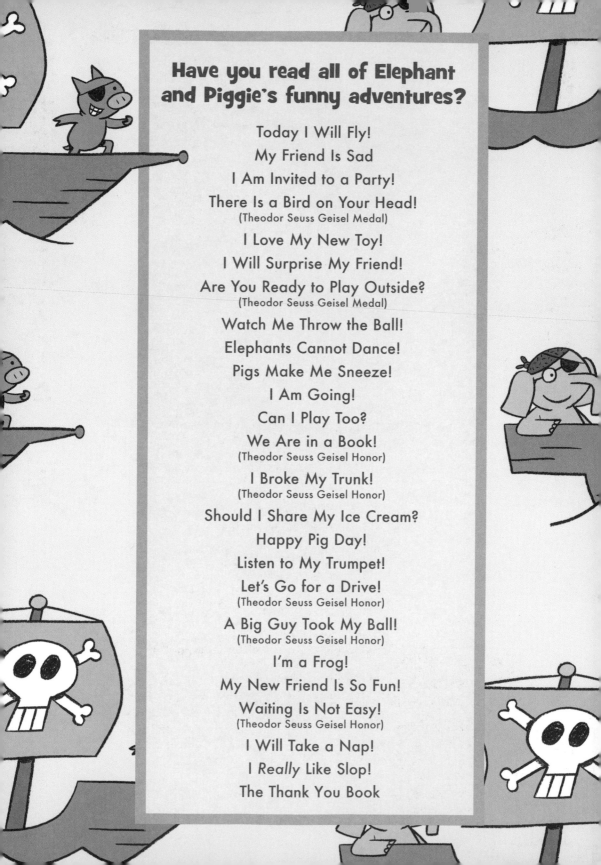

Have you read all of Elephant and Piggie's funny adventures?